Benji Blue

A Robin feeling blue....

Aidan,

Always be proud of who you are!

R McCoy
x

RACHEL MCCOY

To order additional copies of this book, contact:
Xlibris
UK TFN: 0800 0148620 (Toll Free inside the UK)
UK Local: 02036 956328 (+44 20 3695 6328 from outside the UK)
www.xlibrispublishing.co.uk
Orders@ Xlibrispublishing.co.uk

ISBN: Softcover   978-1-6641-1439-5
         EBook   978-1-6641-1438-8

Print information available on the last page

Rev. date: 01/18/2021

For my Mum who taught us to soar.

Benji Blue

Benji Blue was a strange name for a Robin Red Breast but it seemed right for Benji. Benji longed to be like his friends, free to roam and fly, soar and dive but he always had a worry upon his shoulders. He was a loving and caring little bird who loved his family and friends more than anything, but he was not like his friends. They shared stories about their mum and dad and hunting trips they had together. Their nests seemed so different to Benji's but he did not like to tell anyone his secret.

One day Benji was singing on the old oak tree and Charlie and Betty flew over to join him. 'Good morning Benji,' they tweeted together.

'Good morning Betty, good morning Charlie. How are you today?'

'We're great thanks, we 've just been out catching worms with mum and dad,' replied Charlie.

'Have you been out this morning?' chirped Betty.

'Yes,' Benji replied faintly.

Benji began to grow nervous and when he looked down, his beautiful red breast was beginning to turn a light shade of blue. Benji could feel his heart beginning to race and his poor tummy beginning to do somersaults.

'Benji, why is your chest turning a funny blue colour?' asked Betty suspiciously.

'What is wrong with you?' chuckled Charlie.

Benji couldn't help it, the more the other birds laughed, the darker his poor chest began to glow.

Nobody could understand how Benji was feeling. He just wanted to be alone. Benji flew sadly through the forest, hoping he would not meet anyone else on the way to his secret tree.

When Benji reached the special tree that helped him gather his thoughts, he couldn't hold it any longer. Benji began to cry quietly. As he sobbed, his poor red breast grew bluer with every tear that trickled down his chest.

Suddenly Walter, the Wise Old Owl appeared, and perched on the branch beside Benji gently. He spread his large wing around Benji's small, quivering shoulders and muttered, 'What is wrong Benji?' Benji was feeling very lonely and worried and decided to share his long hidden secret with the Wise Old Owl. Walter was very kind and loving and might be able to help him. It was worth a try. Anything was worth a try!

Benji took a deep breath and began.' Well, it's just I feel different to all of my friends. They all have a mum and dad to go hunting and flying with and well...... I just have my mum.'

'Why does that make you upset Benji?' replied Owl softly.

'I just want to be like everyone else!' Benji began to cry again softly and tears began to flow down his sombre blue chest once more.

'Benji, can you fly high in the sky?' asked the owl.

'Yes,' answered Benji, quickly leaping from his perch and soaring above the Wise Owl.

'There's nothing wrong with that!' muttered the Wise Old Owl.

'Can you catch a worm?' questioned the Wise Owl.

Without a second thought, Benji swooped down speedily, catching a worm in his beak, munching merrily as he flew back up to meet Owl.

'Amazing!' said the Owl.

The Wise Old Owl thought for a moment and then asked,' Why do you think your beautiful red breast turns blue Benji?'

'Well, it usually happens when my friends are sharing stories about their family trips. I start to worry because I don't have the same stories to share,' replied Benji glumly.

'Why don't you tell them about your trips?' asked the Wise Owl curiously.

Benji began to think about the Wise Old Owl's question carefully. Benji loved his hunting trips with mum and they always soared and swooped with glee as they caught their dinner. Benji had a skillful and loving mother who could catch a worm quicker than anyone else Benji knew. He began to think of all the wonderful times he had shared with his mother and suddenly Benji's chest began to glow redder than ever before. A warm smile spread across Walter's face as he watched Benji's breast radiating brightly. As the wise old owl glided slowly away, he called out, "Always be proud of who you are Benji!"

When Benji arrived the birds were happily chirping. Benji flew down and landed beside Betty.

Benji glanced down at his tummy full of dread in case it was turning blue. He closed his eyes and thought of the Wise Old Owl and what he had said. He took a deep breath and began to tell his friends about his wonderful trips with his mum and to his amazement, his chest was a beautiful shade of red. He told them how his mum would tell stories as they flew and how she made Benji laugh so hard his tummy wobbled in and out.

To Benji's surprise, the birds gathered around, including the birds from the chestnut tree. They listened so carefully, Benji couldn't even hear the humming of the grass hoppers. Benji told them of his mother's patient and careful approach and the circle began to light up with a red glow. Benji was so proud and happy to be finally sharing one of his special stories, and to his amazement, his friends cheered and tweeted with wonder and interest. As his red breast began to glow redder and redder, Betty shouted, 'Benji, look at your wonderful red breast! It is so bright!'

From that day on, Benji told stories of his flying lessons and hunting trips with pride and he always remembered to be proud of who he was!

THE END

For all those who sometimes feel blue!